Squirrel's World

Lisa Moser

illustrated by Valeri Gorbachev

CANDLEWICK PRESS

For Lydia, because she truly loves all animals.
With much love,
Mom

To Sarah Aliza
V. G.

Text copyright © 2007 by Lisa Moser
Illustrations copyright © 2007 by Valeri Gorbachev

First paperback edition 2008

The Library of Congress has cataloged the hardcover edition as follows:

Moser, Lisa.
Squirrel's world / Lisa Moser ; illustrated by Valeri Gorbachev. —1st ed.
p.   cm.
Summary: Squirrel's well-meaning attempts to help
his forest friends do not always turn out as planned.
ISBN 978-0-7636-2929-8 (hardcover)
[1. Squirrels—Fiction. 2. Forest animals—Fiction. 3. Helpfulness—Fiction.
4. Animals—Fiction. 5. Humorous stories.]   I. Gorbachev, Valeri, ill. II. Title.
PZ7.M84696Squ 2007
[Fic]—dc22   2007060859

ISBN 978-0-7636-4088-0 (paperback)

09 10 11 12 13 TWPS 10 9 8 7 6 5 4 3 2

Printed in Singapore

This book was typeset in Clarendon.
The illustrations were done in ink and watercolor.

Candlewick Press
99 Dover Street
Somerville, Massachusetts 02144

visit us at www.candlewick.com

Contents

Chapter 1
A BUSY, BUSY, BUSY START

Squirrel was busy, busy, busy.

He had to help his tree. "Grow, grow, grow!" cheered Squirrel.

He had to help the river. "Flow, flow, flow!" said Squirrel.

He had to help his friends. "Got to go. Got to go. Got to go, go, go!"

Squirrel found Mouse running up and down a hill.

"Hello, hello, hello!" said Squirrel. "What are you doing?"

"I'm getting food," said Mouse. "I'm storing it in my nest." She put one piece of corn in an old stump.

"Oh boy, oh boy, oh boy!" said Squirrel. "I am a great corn picker. I will help you." He ran up the hill to the cornfield.

"That was a long way," said Squirrel. "I don't want to run up and down. I have an idea."

Squirrel picked ten ears of corn. He rolled them down the hill. "Here they come!" he shouted.

BANG!

THUD!

CRASH!

Squirrel ran down the hill. "Mouse! Mouse! Where are you?"

"Under here," said Mouse.

Squirrel moved the pile. Mouse rubbed her head. She went into her nest in the stump. "Thank you for your help. You can go now."

"No, no, no!" said Squirrel. "I want to help. What other food do you like, like, like?"

"Well," said Mouse, "I like apples."

"Oh boy, oh boy, oh boy!" said Squirrel.
"I am a great apple picker." He ran up a tree.

"I only need one apple!" Mouse shouted.

But Squirrel did not hear. He shook a
branch. An apple fell.

PLUNK. He shook the branch again.

PLUNK.

PLUNK.

PLUNK.

He shook the branch as hard as he could.

PLUNK.

PLUNK.

PLUNK.

PLUNK.

PLUNK.

Squirrel looked down. "Mouse! Mouse!

Where are you?"

PLUNK.

Mouse crawled out of the stump. "I am in here. It was raining apples."

Squirrel looked around. He saw piles and piles of apples. He saw piles and piles of corn. "It will take you forever to eat all this food," said Squirrel.

"Yes, it will," said Mouse.

"Hooray!" said Squirrel. "Tomorrow I will come back to help, help, help."

Squirrel jumped from tree to tree.

"Got to go.

   Got to go.

      Got to go, go, go!" said Squirrel.

Mouse rested against an apple.

Chapter 2
THE PERFECT GAME

Squirrel went to the river.

"Hello, hello, hello!" said Squirrel. "Is that you, Turtle?"

Turtle looked at his feet. Turtle looked at his shell. "Yup. It's me," said Turtle.

"What are you doing?" asked Squirrel.

"I was playing a game," said Turtle. "But I fell asleep."

"Oh boy, oh boy, oh boy!" said Squirrel. "I am a great game player. I will help you."

Squirrel jumped over Turtle's nose.

Turtle did not move.

BOING!

Squirrel jumped over Turtle's shell.

Turtle did not move.

BOING!

Squirrel jumped over Turtle's tail.

Turtle did not move.

BOING!

BOING!

BOING!

BOING!

Squirrel jumped and jumped and jumped.

Then he looked at Turtle. "You are not good at this game," he said.

"What are we playing?" asked Turtle.

"I am playing Leap, Leap, Leapfrog," said Squirrel. "But you are playing Sleep, Sleep, Sleepfrog."

"Your game is too fast," said Turtle. "Let's play my slow game. It's called Find a Four-Leaf Clover. First, sit down."

Squirrel sat on his tail.

Squirrel sat on his paws.

Squirrel sat on his head.

Turtle fell asleep.

"Wake up, Turtle," said Squirrel. "I'm sitting down. What's next?"

"Find a clover," said Turtle.

Squirrel found a clover.

Squirrel found a rock.

Squirrel found a dirty old shoe.

Turtle fell asleep.

"Wake up, Turtle," said Squirrel. "I found a clover. What's next?"

"Count the leaves," said Turtle.

Squirrel counted the leaves.

Squirrel counted his paws.

Squirrel counted his teeth.

Turtle fell asleep.

"Wake up, Turtle," said Squirrel. "I have an idea. Let's play a game we both like. Let's play Hide-and-Seek."

"Close your eyes," said Turtle. "I'll hide."

Turtle hid behind an old log. He did not move.

Squirrel ran up a tree
and looked.

He jumped in a bush
and looked.

He looked under a rock.

He looked in a puddle.

At last Squirrel looked behind the old log.
"I found you!" he said.

Turtle looked at his feet. Turtle looked at his shell. "Yup. It's me."

"That was fun, fun, fun!" said Squirrel.

"Yup," said Turtle. "I like to hide. You like to seek. Hide-and-Seek is the perfect game for us."

Squirrel patted Turtle's back.

"Got to go.

   Got to go.

      Got to go, go, go!" said Squirrel.

Turtle fell asleep.

Chapter 3

ONE WET RABBIT

Squirrel found Rabbit by the pond.

"Hello, hello, hello!" said Squirrel. "What are you doing?"

Rabbit looked at some dark clouds. His ears trembled. His whiskers twitched. "I need that leaf." Rabbit pointed to a lily pad in the pond. "But I do not like to get wet."

"Oh boy, oh boy, oh boy!" said Squirrel. "I am a great leaf getter. I will help you."

Squirrel ran into the woods. He came back with a big stick. "I am going to whack, whack, whack that leaf! Then it will float to shore."

SMACK went the stick.

SPLASH went the water.

"Oh, dear!" said Rabbit.

SMACK went the stick.

SPLASH went the water.

"Oh, no!" said Rabbit.

Water dripped from Rabbit's nose.

Water dripped from Rabbit's ears.

Water dripped from Rabbit's tail.

"Oh boy, oh boy, oh boy!" said Squirrel.

"I have another idea."

Rabbit looked up. The clouds were darker.
A cold wind blew. "Please hurry!" said Rabbit.

Squirrel pushed a log into the water. "We will
go out on the log. I will reach, reach, reach.
I will get that leaf."

"Pardon me," said Rabbit. "Last time I got wet.
May I try this time?"

Rabbit and Squirrel went out on the log.
Rabbit leaned over.

"You are close, close, close!" cheered Squirrel.
He jumped up and down on the log. Rabbit
wobbled a little.

Rabbit leaned more.

"You are closer, closer, closer!" cheered Squirrel. He jumped up, down, up, down on the log. Rabbit wobbled a lot.

Rabbit leaned way over. He grabbed the lily pad and pulled.

"You've got it, got it, got it!" yelled Squirrel. He jumped up, down, up, down, up, down.

The log went up, down, up, down, up, down. Rabbit fell into the water.

SPLASH!

Squirrel pulled Rabbit out of the water.

Water dripped from Rabbit's nose.

Water dripped from Rabbit's ears.

Water dripped from Rabbit's tail.

"What will you do with that leaf, leaf, leaf?"

asked Squirrel.

Rabbit held the lily pad over his head.

Raindrops began to fall. "It is an umbrella,"

said Rabbit. "I do not like to get wet."

Squirrel danced in the rain.

"Got to go.

Got to go.

Got to go, go, go!" said Squirrel.

Rabbit waved good-bye from under his lily pad.

Chapter 4

GOOD, GOOD, GOOD NIGHT

Squirrel ran up to his nest. He stretched out on some old leaves. "It has been a good, good, good day," said Squirrel. He closed his eyes.

Suddenly he jumped up. "Oh, oh, oh!" said Squirrel. "I forgot to say good night."

Squirrel ran to the old stump.

He yelled, "Mouse! Mouse!"

"What?" squeaked Mouse.

"What are you doing, doing, doing?"
asked Squirrel.

"Sleeping," said Mouse.

"I came to say good, good, good night."

Mouse sighed. "Good night, Squirrel."

"Now go to sleep," said Squirrel.

Squirrel found Turtle at the river, counting stars.

"You should be sleeping, sleeping, sleeping," said Squirrel.

"I'm not tired," said Turtle.

"Oh boy, oh boy, oh boy!" said Squirrel. "I have an idea. Counting sheep will make you tired."

"Yup," said Turtle. "But I don't have any sheep."

"I will help you," said Squirrel.

Squirrel started bouncing.

"Baa, baa, baa," he said.

He bounced up a tree.

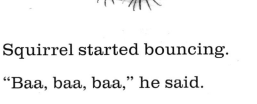

"Baa, baa, baa."

"Baa, baa, baa."

He bounced on a rock.

"Baa, baa, baa."

He bounced on Turtle's shell.

"Are you sleepy, sleepy, sleepy?" asked Squirrel.

"Nope," said Turtle. "Just dizzy from watching you."

"I have another idea," said Squirrel. "You could count stars instead."

"Yup," said Turtle. He sat down and started counting.

Squirrel found Rabbit in his burrow.

"What are you doing, doing, doing?" asked Squirrel.

"I am trying not to be afraid," said Rabbit. His ears trembled. His whiskers twitched.

"Afraid of what?" asked Squirrel.

"The dark," whispered Rabbit.

"I have an idea," said Squirrel. He ran outside.

A big, lumpy shadow walked toward Rabbit.

Rabbit yelled, "Squirrel, help me! I'm scared!"

"It's only me, me, me," said Squirrel.

He opened his paw. A firefly glowed brightly.
"Now you won't have to be afraid of the dark,"
said Squirrel.

Rabbit gently took the firefly. "I will take good
care of him," said Rabbit. "Thank you. You have
been a big help."

"You are welcome, welcome, welcome," said
Squirrel.

Squirrel ran back to his nest. He snuggled in some old leaves.

"It has been a good,

good,

good day," said Squirrel.

Then he finally went to sleep.

8